2

2

Come Home Already!

By Jory John
Illustrated by Benji Davies

HarperCollins *Children's Books*

First published by HarperCollins Children's Books, a division of HarperCollins Publishers, USA, in 2017
First published in hardback in Great Britain by HarperCollins Children's Books in 2018

1 3 5 7 9 10 8 6 4 2

ISBN: 978-0-00-827685-0

HarperCollins Children's Books is a division of HarperCollins Publishers Ltd.

Text copyright © Jory John 2017
Illustrations copyright © Benji Davies 2017

Visit our website at www.harpercollins.co.uk

Printed and bound in China

To Sam Barkin, who always
brings the fun.
—Jory John

For Rohan, the explorer.
—Benji Davies

"I wonder what ol' Bear is up to. . ."

"Get ready for some more fun times, Bear!"

KNOCK KNOCK

"And I won't take no for an answer. . ."

"Wait a minute. . ."

"Bear's gone fishing?
He's back next week?

BEAR'S GONE FISHING?
HE'S BACK NEXT WEEK?

He's gone fishing?
Without me?
But...
but...

NEXT WEEK?!

FISHING?!

What am I going to do with myself until then?!"

"Ah, yes. This is the life. Alone with my thoughts. No pesky neighbours knocking on my door at all hours. It's nice to be by myself for once. Ahhhhhhhhhhhh."

"Hmmm..."

"It's okay.

It's all right.

It's not even a big deal.

So Bear left without me and I'm all alone.

I'll be fine! Ha ha! Yes!
Ha!
Ha!
Ha!
I'm just fine!

After all, I can entertain myself!"

No. . . I'll play my drums!

No. . . I'll watch a movie!

No. . . I'll read!

Wait, I already said that."

"Sigh. I really don't feel like doing any of these things. I miss my friend."

"COME HOME ALREADY, BEAR!"

"I'm just so bored! I wonder what ol' Bear is doing right this second. I bet he's having so much fun without me."

"Ugh. There's got to be an easier way to set up a tent. Ah, never mind. I'll figure it out later. Time for some fishing."

"Oh. Darn. It's starting to rain. I don't like to get my fur wet."

"I haven't caught a single fish. And I forgot to bring snacks. I miss my refrigerator."

"I'm drenched. I'm hungry. I don't know how to start a campfire. And I'm just so tired."

"There's really only one thing to do. I have to catch up with Bear. He'll surely need my help. After all, I know how to catch fish with my beak.

Also, I'm great company!

Fishing can be really lonely.

Plus it's raining."

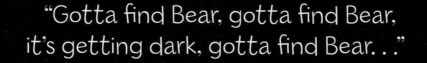

"Gotta find Bear, gotta find Bear,
it's getting dark, gotta find Bear..."

"The woods are scary at night. What was that noise?! It was probably nothing. Think about other things, Bear. Just think about other things."

"Nothing to worry about here.
Nothing to worry about at all. . ."

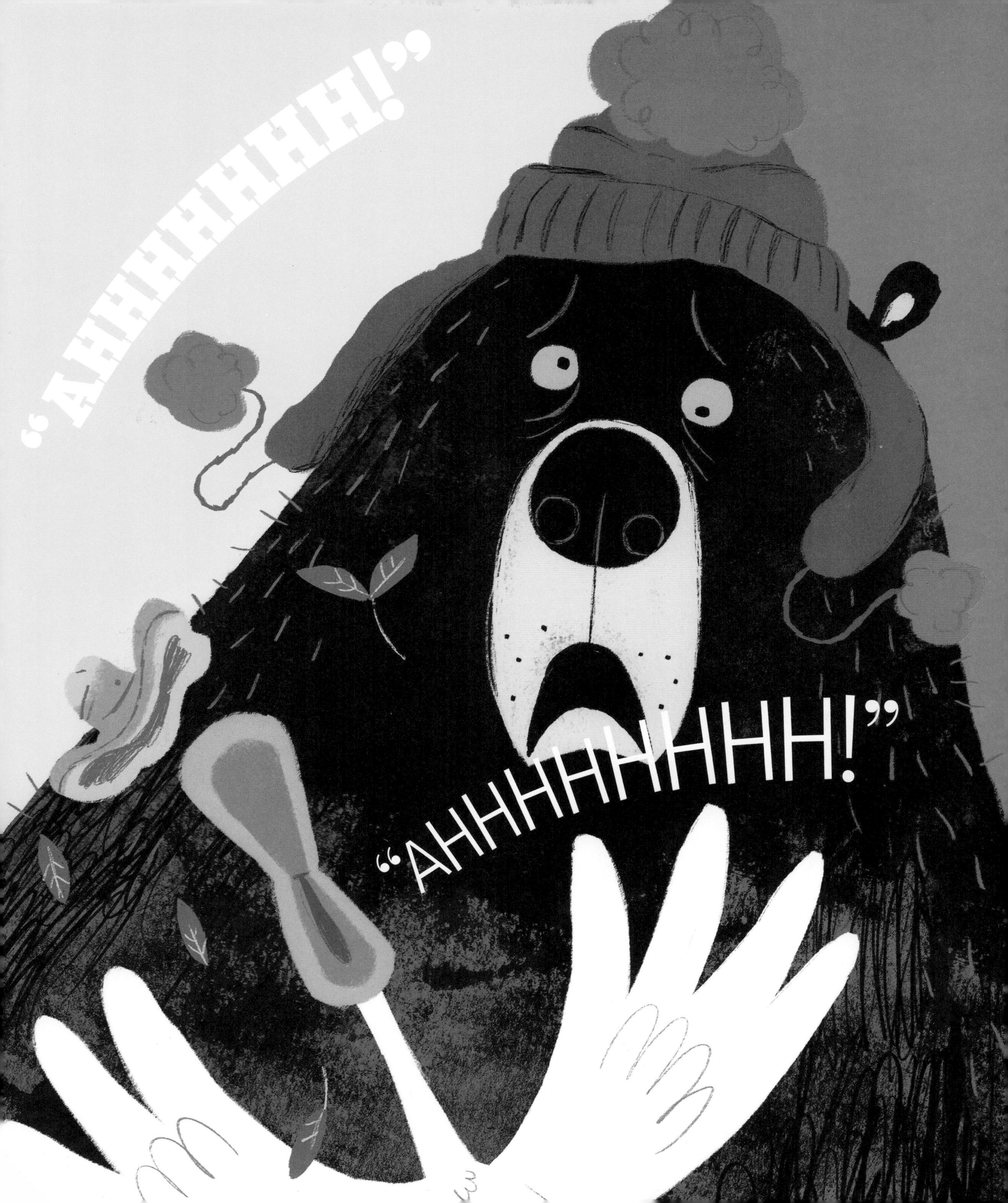
"AHHHHHHHH!"
"AHHHHHHHHH!"

"Bear! It's me. Duck! From next door. I found you, ol' buddy, ol' pal, ol' chum. Are you hungry? Are you cold?
Are you scared?
Why were you screaming?
Why was I screaming?"

"Duck? Duck? Is it really you? How did you find me?"

"I wanted you to come home, so I tracked you through the woods. I missed you. Come home already, Bear!"

"Duck, I'm actually SO relieved to see you!"

"You are?"

"Absolutely! Please stay. Keep me company. We can go back home together in the morning."

"That sounds wonderful, Bear! Perfect. Sublime. I actually thought you wanted to get away from me."

"Let me help you get set up. I'm good at building tents and making fires, and we can roast these marshmallows I brought. Camping is much better with a friend, Bear."

"Yes. I can see that, Duck."

"So, before I found you. . . did you catch any fish at all, Bear?"

"No."

"Did you enjoy the rain?"

"No."

"Did you have fun?"

"No."

"Did you make any friends?"

"No."

"Did you catch any fish?"

"You already said that."

"Well, I'm very glad you're home, Bear. Next time you want to go camping, give me a ring. I'll come along. I'll always be by your side, Bear. Always and forever."

"Always and forever? Sigh."